P9-CAA-529

The Queen of COLORS

For my sisters

The Queen of Colors

Jutta Bauer

North
South

One morning, Queen Matilda stepped out of her castle.

BLUE!

She summoned her subjects.

Along came Blue.

It was soft and gentle. It said a nice
hello to Matilda and colored the sky.

Then it colored the queen and quietly disappeared.

Next, Matilda called Red.

It almost knocked her over.

She ordered it to turn into a horse,

and they went riding through the kingdom.

Red was wild and did dangerous things.
Matilda also felt wild and dangerous.

But finally she had had enough
and ordered Red to leave.

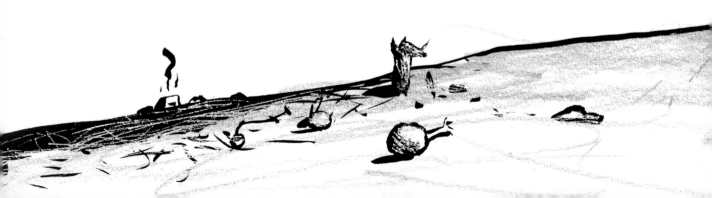

It stayed a bit pink but not for long,
because now Yellow arrived.

"Stay here!" she commanded.
"You're so warm and bright."

But Yellow was not only warm and bright. It could be bad mannered and bad tempered as well.

So could Matilda, and very soon they quarreled.

Gentle Blue wanted to keep the peace but had
no success, and Red came along to see what was
going on. Gradually everything turned gray.

And grayer.

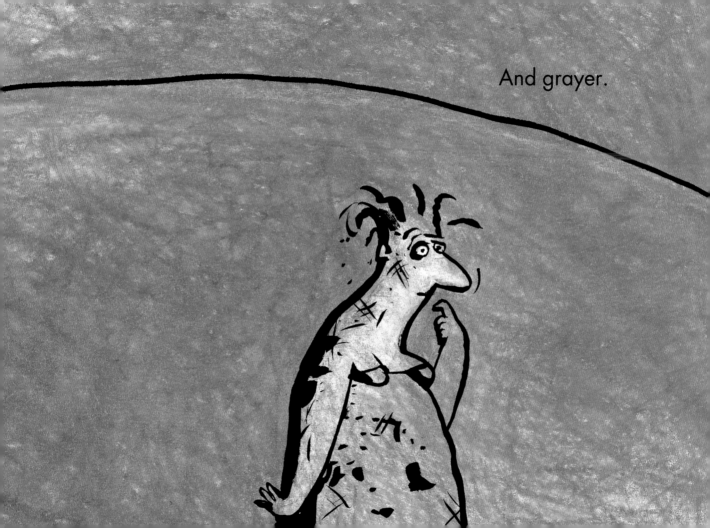

And grayer.

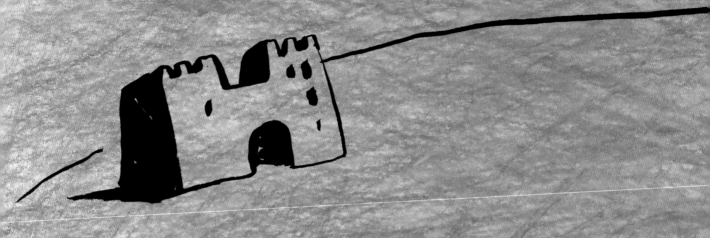

Matilda turned gray, the castle turned gray,

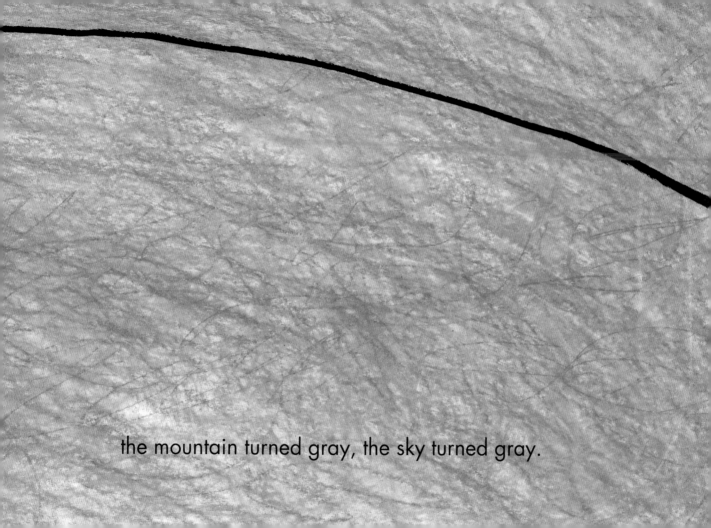

the mountain turned gray, the sky turned gray.

"Go away!" shouted Matilda.

She stomped her feet and screamed.

Gray wasn't prepared to be ordered
around. It stayed where it was.
A long time passed.

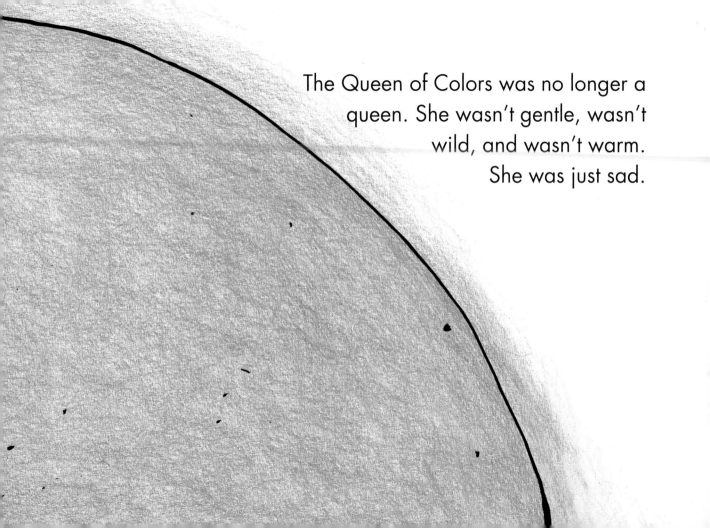

The Queen of Colors was no longer a
queen. She wasn't gentle, wasn't
wild, and wasn't warm.
She was just sad.

Then Matilda started to cry.

At first her crying was faint and quiet,

but soon it became stronger and louder.

Tears streamed down her cheeks,
and the more tears she shed,
the more Gray was washed away.

There were tears everywhere.

And suddenly, the colors were there again: soft Blue,

wild Red, warm and sometimes bad tempered Yellow.

Now they all played together . . .

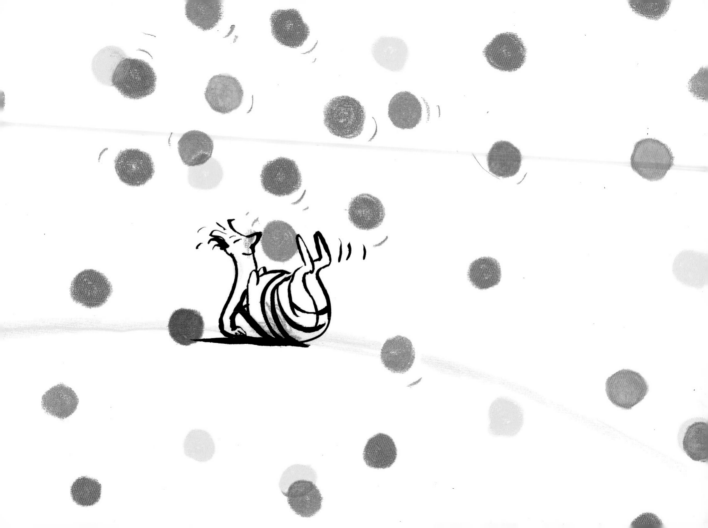

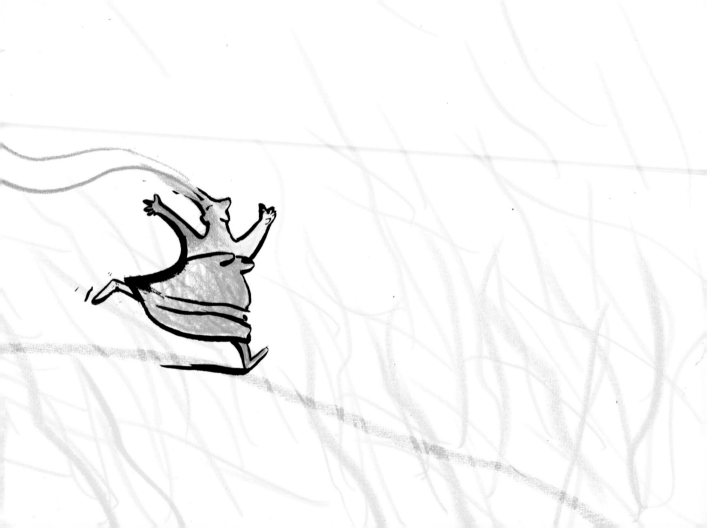

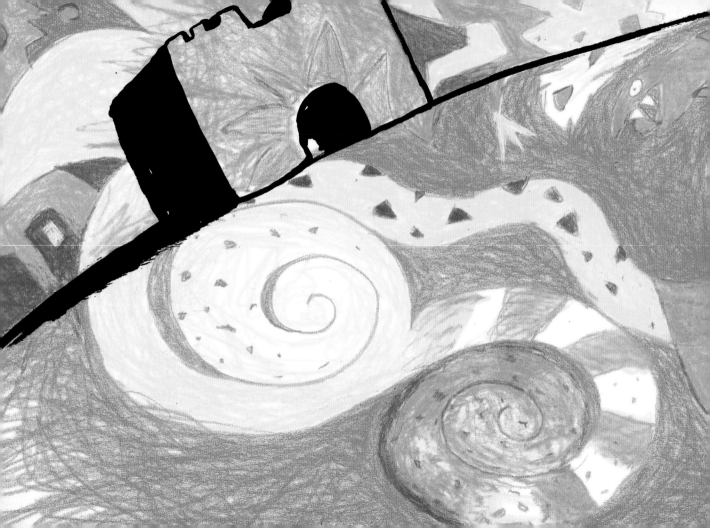

. . . until they began to feel tired.

Then soft Blue covered up everything.

Here you can do your own coloring.

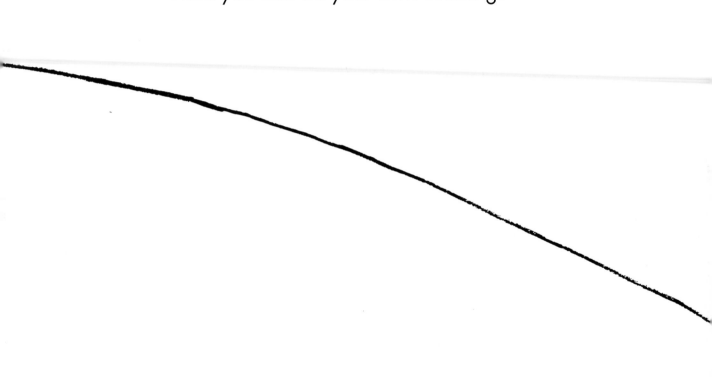

First published in the United States and Canada in 2014 by NorthSouth Books, Inc.,
an imprint of NordSüd Verlag AG, CH-8005 Zürich, Switzerland.

Distributed in the United States by NorthSouth Books Inc., New York 10016.
Library of Congress Cataloging-in-Publication Data is available.
ISBN: 978-0-7358-4166-6 (trade edition)
Printed in China by Leo Paper Products Ltd., Kowloon Bay, Hong Kong, January 2014.
1 3 5 7 9 • 10 8 6 4 2
www.northsouth.com

Jutta Bauer, born in 1955 in Hamburg, is a German writer and illustrator. She studied at the Technical School of Design in Hamburg. She has illustrated numerous children's books as well as written her own stories and today is one of the most renowned picture book artists in Germany. Her book *Schreimutter (Screaming Mother)*, which she wrote and illustrated, was honored with the German Youth Literary Award. For her "lasting contribution" as a children's book illustrator, she received the Hans Christian Andersen Medal in 2010. Jutta Bauer has a son and lives in Germany.

Die Königin der Farben (The Queen of Colors), first produced as a film for television, is regarded as one of the most beautiful films for children, receiving the German Youth Literary Award for excellence. In addition, it has received many children's book prizes, from the North Rhine-Westphalia Award to the Troisdorfer Picture Book Prize, and is aired every year on Radio Bremen.